BLANKET CHECK

MEYARI MCFARLAND

CONTENTS

Other Books by Meyari McFarland:	v
Blanket Check	1
Author's Note: The Shores of Twilight Bay	12
1. Cloudy Arrival	13
2. Mossy Path	21
Other Books by Meyari McFarland:	29
Afterword	31
Author Bio	33

SPECIAL OFFER

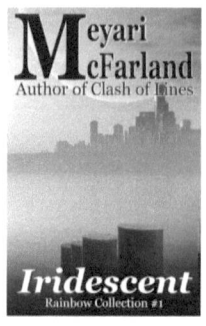

Special Offer

The rainbow has infinite shades, just as this collection covers the spectrum of fictional possibilities.

From contemporary romances like *The Shores of Twilight Bay* to dark fantasy like *A Lone Red Tree* and out to SF futures in *Child of Spring*, *Iridescent* covers the gamut of time, space and genre.

Meyari McFarland shows her mastery in this first omnibus collection of her short fiction. Twenty-five amazing stories, all with queer characters going on adventures, solving mysteries, and falling in love are here in the first Rainbow Collection.

And now you can get this massive collection of short queer fiction, all of it with the happy endings you love, *for free!*

Sign up here for your free copy of Iridescent now!

OTHER BOOKS BY MEYARI MCFARLAND:

Day Hunt on the Final Oblivion
Day of Joy
Immortal Sky

A New Path
Following the Trail
Crafting Home
Finding a Way
Go Between
Like Arrows of Fate

Out of Disaster

The Shores of Twilight Bay

Coming Together
Following the Beacon
The Solace of Her Clan

You can find these and many other books at www.MDR-Publishing.com. We are a small independent publisher focusing on LGBT content. Please sign up for our mailing list to get regular updates on the latest preorders and new releases and a free ebook!

Copyright ©2024 by Mary Raichle

Print ISBN: 978-1-64309-114-3

Cover image

©okanakdeniz on DepositePhotos ID# 92952778

All rights reserved. No part of this publication may be reproduced or transmitted in any form or by any means, electronic or mechanical, including photocopy, recording or any information storage and retrieval system, without permission in writing from the publisher.

Requests for permission to make copies of any part of the work should be emailed to publisher@mdr-publishing.com.

This book is also available in TPB format from all major retailers.

❦ Created with Vellum

This story is dedicated to my husband who can't go boating but who loves the Puget Sound as much as I do.

BLANKET CHECK

Martie hummed as the brisk sea wind blew through her hair. She'd pulled off her sparkly pink beanie when the ferry pulled away from the dock despite the cold nipping her nose and ears. Her cheeks felt chapped from the breeze but that didn't stop her from grinning at the seagulls coasting overhead. Tiny white clouds scudded by way, way up in the sky. They looked like lambs scampering across a blue field.

The delightful block of a ferry out of Anacortes would take Martie and her twin Artie through the Puget Sound's many islands to Orcas Island. Once there, Storm would be waiting with her slow old speedboat with its rainbow patches so that they could make the trip out to tiny little Blanket Island where they'd be spending the week.

It'd been years since Martie had been able to come on one of these trips. PHDs were hell on taking time off, especially when you were on scholarship. She'd had to work every single week for ages and ages and ages. On the other hand, Storm went every single summer, no exceptions. She'd gotten thoroughly red in the face last week when Martie had suggested, tongue firmly in cheek, that maybe, just possibly, for once, they might go somewhere else.

"We always go to the Island!" Storm had spluttered, hands flying as she signed with big looping gestures full of aggravation and fear that everyone would agree with Martie. "It's tradition! Besides, it's cheap. No rent because my family owns the darn thing. We just bring food and whatever booze you guys want and we're set. Come on, you can't really…"

Outraged was a gorgeous look on Storm. Her normally pale skin went all rosy and her dark eyes snapped as she stared at Martie. She'd shaved her hair off since the last time Martie had seen her, leaving her scalp with black peach fuzz that Martie was desperately curious to rub her hands over.

Storm's hands had spluttered to a stop as Martie had started giggling. Artie swatted at Martie's shoulder, which, deserved. Honestly deserved. Not that it'd stopped Artie from grinning and fist-bumping Martie.

"You two are The Worst," Storm had huffed while glaring at both of them. "Official T.M. damn you. You're gonna give Tracey ideas."

Both Tracey and Lake, cuddled together on Storm's huge leather sofa, had snickered and shaken their head solemnly. Monthly get-togethers in person were hard since they'd all, other than Martie darn it, graduated college. It was rare for Tracey and Lake to make it but then they did have their brand-new baby Nat to take care of along with their shop selling candles, candies and cool things.

That was still a way better store name than boring old Van Norup Sundries and Novelties.

"We've got my sisters covering us for the week," Tracey had said. "We are so going. It'll be Nat's first time on the Island. Martie's just winding you up. Again. You make it way too easy, Storm."

The next huff of outrage had Storm throwing up her hands as she flopped back into her leopard-print beanbag.

Martie grinned as she leaned on the ferry's cold steel railing. Winding Storm up was and would always be one of her favorite things. It was far too much fun.

A poke in the left kidney startled Martie. She turned and grinned at Artie, her twin. He had both their suitcases with the handles waving up in the air like a kid with her hand raised. Hers was pink tiger-striped, his solid purple. Martie tucked her suitcase between her feet and bounced on her toes while wagging her eyebrows at Artie.

Where Martie had let her hair fly free and her face go rosy with the cold, Artie was securely wrapped up in his jacket with a scarf covering everything from his eyes down. His beanie was deep purple with an extravagantly huge pompom on top that fluttered in the wind.

"You're in a good mood," Artie signed.

"We get to see Storm," Martie signed back, grinning and bouncing. "For a whole week!"

Artie shook his head, eyes smiling though his hands were serious-steady instead of teasing. "One of these days, Storm is going to haul off and smack you for teasing her."

"Oh, poo, she will not," Martie signed, rolling her eyes when Artie shook his head again. "Seriously, she knows I'm just playing around. It's fine. That's what friends do, you know?"

"If you say so," Artie signed with so much droll resignation that Martie just about demanded to know what he was fussing over.

But nope, no time for interrogations that Artie would ignore with all the calm of a completely deaf person who didn't care if you get red in the face trying to catch his attention. She'd had him pretend she wasn't there while she sat in his lap and made faces at him. Not since they were in high school, sure, but Artie was like that. If he didn't want to answer a question, there was no answer coming.

Darn it.

Not that it mattered. The ferry chugged towards Orcas Island's southern dock with seagulls screeching all around them. No one else was out on the prow. Too windy, too cold. Wusses. It wasn't that cold.

Martie shoved her hands in her pockets as the ferry angled its butt so that the car ramp under her and Artie would line up with the big green-painted steel dock. There was a nice line of cars waiting to get onto the ferry for the return trip to Anacortes. No one was standing out on the pedestrian ramp, just like no one was outside on the prow with her and Martie.

Their loss. This whole sidle up and let the cars off thing was awesome. Kind of like watching a marsupial open its pouch. Or something.

She craned her neck towards the dock off to the left of the ferry terminal. No sign of Storm but then at this angle Martie wasn't likely to see anything. When she checked the second, fourth and ninth time, she still couldn't see anything.

"Stop it," Artie signed.

"Just checking," Martie protested with her best innocent look.

"You literally can't see Storm from here," Artie signed, glaring at her. "You know this. It's not changed since you went into the PHD program, Martie."

Martie sulked, turtling down in her coat as the ferry finally docked and then dropped the gate for the cars. Thirty seconds later, a crew member marched out and unlocked the gate for pedestrians. Forever and a half! Would it have hurt them to have someone out here so that they could get going right away?

The crew member barely got out of the way of Martie's

suitcase. She would've run ahead but Artie snagged her elbow and kept Martie from rushing off to see if Storm was there or not. Which meant she was stuck with a long, slow stroll up the pedestrian ramp to the shore, through the red-roofed terminal. Artie didn't even let her run down the road along the shore to the pier past the boat charter place and it's too-expensive, not-very-good restaurant. He didn't even react as Martie groaned and rolled her eyes at not being able to run right through the little hoard of tourists cluttering up the pier.

Artie only relented and let Martie go when they finally reached the steel ramp that led from the pier down to the private boat dock. Probably, knowing Artie's bone-deep troll tendencies, the only reason he let her go was that Storm was there with her battered old speedboat, bouncing and waving from behind the wheel.

She'd put on a proper cable-knitted hat in black wool with big chunky cables that made it look like she'd not cut her hair. They looked more like cornrows than a hat from a distance. Martie's heart skipped a beat as she grinned and waved urgently back at Storm.

"Storm!" Martie shouted as she ran down the ramp dragging her suitcase. "It's such a pretty day! I'm surprised no one else came to meet us."

Storm snorted and grabbed Martie's suitcase before she could accidentally drop it in the ocean. "Honey, it's a good twenty degrees colder than normal. Everyone's freezing. Even me. Where's your hat? And why is your face so red? You weren't out on the front of ferry the whole way, were you?"

"Eh, it wasn't that cold," Martie said, waving a hand just in time for Artie to shove his suitcase past her to Storm. "I'm fine."

"She was out on the prow the whole time, wasn't she?"

Storm signed to Artie as soon as she stowed his suitcase in the back seat of her speedboat.

"Yeah," Artie signed so sadly that it took on an overly dramatic sigh.

"Get in the boat," Storm huffed at Martie.

She gave Artie a hand in, making sure that he was snug between the two suitcases with a nice waterproof blanket over his legs. Artie snuggled down in it like a clam burying itself in the mud. Martie shook her head. He wasn't going to even try to figure out what they said on the way to Blanket Island, not with his hands buried that deep under the blanket.

Which meant that Martie could bend Storm's ear the whole way there.

Yay!

The instant that Martie was in the boat, in her seat, Storm untied them and started carefully backing them out of the slip. She was always very careful with her speedboat, probably because her uncle who'd left it to her had been so brutally casual about damaging the poor thing.

"Any new leaks?" Martie asked once they'd gotten turned around and headed out into the Puget Sound heading west towards Blanket Island.

"Not on the boat," Storm replied with a groaning laugh that Martie grinned at. "That darn well house has another leak in the roof. Tracey got right up there working to fix it even though Lake pitched a fit. I'm hoping we get back before Tracey gets it all done. You know how she is. She'll keep working on the zillion and ten things that need fixing."

"It's Tracey," Martie said. "That's her thing."

Something that had been tense and unhappy for the last few years started to relax as the wind picked up once they were out of the speed-controlled zone around Orcas Island. The clouds overhead had changed from fluffy little lambs to big huge rams that jumbled up together until, as they rounded the point at Orcas Village, they turned into a rumpled white blanket over the sky.

The seagulls that had welcomed the ferry peeled off as Storm guided her speedboat out to the west between the bulk of Shaw Island and Crane Island. Their screeches dimmed and died, leaving Martie with the roar of the engine and the splash of the waves as they zipped across the ocean.

"I missed this," Martie admitted once they were well and truly on their way.

"The wind and cold?" Storm asked, amusement making her side-eye Martie.

"Oh, yeah," Martie said, grinning and snort-laughing when one of Storm's eyebrows went up. "No, silly. The Island. Taking time off. Seeing all of you and just, you know, relaxing. I've been way too busy with the stupid PHD."

Storm nodded, both hands on the wheel as she looked where they were going instead of at Martie. "We understood, you know? It's a ton of work. You did it all without loans, just scholarships and way too much work. I'm not the only one who's just... full of admiration that you made it."

"That was not being able to afford any more loans after my Masters," Martie groaned. "But thanks. It's nice to know everyone respects my ability to throw myself into stupid decisions and then stand my ground like a moron."

It came out way too bitter. Way, way too bitter. Storm side-eyed Martie again before sighing.

"Didn't get that job you wanted?" Storm asked.

"Nope," Martie said.

"Bummer."

Which was all Storm said. That was one of the best things about Storm. When Martie told Artie he'd been all up in the "try applying here" and "change this on your resume", like advice was what Martie really needed. It wasn't. At all.

She'd wanted someone, Storm preferably, to hear, understand, and sympathize.

And that's exactly what Storm did. Because Storm was awesome and the best person in the world and more fun to be with than even Artie after three beers.

Artie was such a lightweight.

The space between the islands felt like it was as big as the entire Pacific as they flew along through the Wasp Passage between Crane and Shaw Islands. Martie smiled and breathed in the, honestly, frigid air. Green pine and moss-covered elm blanketed the shores on either side. The water was a lovely paler sapphire here with deep dark cobalt blue up ahead where the water deepened out on the other side of the Passage.

Blanket Island, their little home away from home rested off to the north once they were fully through the passage. Storm smiled along with Martie as she turned the wheel and sent waves rushing back at Shaw Island's north shore.

"Almost there," Storm commented. "We'll get you all warmed up once we're on dry land."

Martie stared at her as the weight lifting from her shoulders mingled with Artie's comment earlier in the trip. Tracey had teased Martie about needing a Storm fix when she'd been in the shop to pick up another bottle of Martie's favorite custom-scented shampoo. And, well, the last time Martie had felt this good, this happy…

…had been the last time she'd been out to Blanket Island.

With Storm.

They hadn't even been out to stay. One of Storm's cousins had reported that the bunk house had a leak in the kitchen, so Martie had volunteered to help get it fixed. She was a good bit stronger than Storm, after all. All that lifting of epic heavy hardback books for the PHD, you know.

They'd cursed, gotten rained on, cursed a whole bunch

more and gone home soaking, miserable but with the job done.

Martie had enjoyed every single minute.

It was one of a billion times she'd spent with Storm that were a hundred jillion trillion times better just because Storm was there. Practically from the moment they met, Martie had been happier around Storm. Happier, more energetic, more cheerful and driven.

Heck, the only reason she'd gotten the stupid PHD was that Storm had been utterly convinced that Martie was smart enough to do it easily.

God, she was the stupidest smartie-pants on the planet, wasn't she?

"What's got you making that face?" Storm asked as she slowed the engine and guided the speedboat towards Blanket Island's wobbly, half-submerged dock that Lake was very seriously not standing on as she waited for them to pull in.

Something else that needed to be fixed.

"I'm an idiot," Martie declared as she realized *finally* that the "smack" Artie had been talking about might not have been a punch.

"You're the exact opposite of an idiot," Storm said with a snort. "What's inspired this bout of self-doubt?"

Storm tossed the line to Lake on the shore, smiling as Lake tied it to one of the big old cedars that listed over the water like it was drunk. Yeah, that dock really seriously needed to be fixed. At least tying off to the tree got them close enough to the part of the dock that was relatively stable.

Artie got out. He took the suitcases and passed the up to Lake who gleefully hugged him before asking in sign all about the trip here and where Martie's hat was. She very distinctly signed the whole bit about being frozen solid so that Martie couldn't help but see it, much to Artie's snort-laughing amusement.

"I noticed something," Martie said as Storm helped her out of the speedboat and onto the wobbly dock.

"What?" Storm asked.

So, maybe grabbing Storm's face and pulling her over so that Martie could kiss her wasn't the best way to test Martie's realization. The kiss was awkward, noses bumping and teeth clacking together as Storm flailed and the dock wobbled underneath them.

But it was still amazing and perfect and wonderful even with Martie's nose all but burning against the heat of Storm's ferociously blushing cheek.

Martie pulled back and grinned. "That. I finally noticed that. I'm a total idiot for not realizing I was in love with you like, oh, I don't know? A decade ago?"

Storm stared, frozen solid other than her rapidly blinking eyes. She turned to Artie, who was doing a victory dance right out of middle school pee wee football, and Lake, who had her hands over her mouth even though it didn't do a thing to stop the high-pitched squeaks of delight.

"That… you… I…?" Storm spluttered.

"Yes?" Martie asked. She grinned and caught one of Storm's hands. "I mean, yes, you'll date me even though I'm a total moron about relationships? And yes, that was a nice kiss? Awkward and stupid timing but yes? Please?"

Storm started laughing. "Oh God. Yes, you maniac. I will date you. It was amazing. And yes, you're a total dweeb!"

She turned to head up the dock, but her aim was totally off because her foot was about to go off the edge of the dock into the ice-cold water. Martie gasped and hauled on Storm's hand. They teetered and then screamed as the dock lurched, throwing both of them into the water.

Martie came up spluttering and laughing. She caught

Storm, pushed her towards the shore and grinned. Best day on Blanket Island ever, even if they did get dunked and frozen half to death.

At least she finally realized her heart was right in front of her the whole time.

AUTHOR'S NOTE: THE SHORES OF TWILIGHT BAY

The Puget Sound has a lot of little islands. The waterways between them are beautiful, full of sword ferns draped down to the water's edge, cedar trees looming and orca swimming under the surface. It's a lovely, magical place to visit, especially if you can get down on the water and see everything.

So it's no surprise that I've written several stories set in the little islands of the Puget Sound. The Shores of Twilight Bay is another one, with more girls falling in love while surrounded by the beauty of nature. And the cold, of course. But that's half the fun. The other half is exploring and seeing what you can learn, about the place and the people you're with.

Hope you enjoy the sample!

1. CLOUDY ARRIVAL

Tai bounced on her toes, the dock rocking underneath her. Icy cold water washed up over her shoes, dampening her socks and sending chills up her spine. Such a cold day. May wasn't supposed to be this cold but here she was, standing on the dock with a winter coat, wet shoes and hands that felt like ice cubes.

If the lilacs weren't blooming she'd think it was March.

Honestly, though, you could barely tell that the lilacs were in bloom today. The grape-clusters of blossoms had clamped shut when faced with the cold weather. Her head should be swimming from the drunk-inducing smell of the things lurking by the dock and instead all she could smell was seaweed, that rotting fish up the shore and the snap of salt from the Sound.

Not exactly the best welcome for her friends. Definitely not what she'd intended when she invited them all out for a week-long vacation away from the world. Having your own island, little though it was, in the middle of the Puget Sound was an awesome, awesome thing. During the summer. When winter came around it was a lot less enticing to come out and stay for a while. The way the weather was going, Xinyi's new girlfriend was going to think that it was always rainy, windy and cold here.

If only they'd arrived yesterday when the sun was shining, the water was still as glass and Tai had been wandering around in board shorts and nothing else. No need for anything more around here. The nearest people were miles away and on the other side of the island from Tai's cabin. She could go topless all she wanted.

Well.

She could. She generally didn't. The thought of someone sailing by tended to send her running for the cabin, hands clamped over her teeny-tiny boobs. But she'd been daring and done it yesterday and now it was winter again.

Damn the weather anyway.

Still, they should have fun, once the others got here. Tai had come early so that she could make sure everything was ready. All the food they could eat in a solid month, nice clean sheets, tons of games. She'd made sure that the kayaks were all cleaned up and ready, that the paddles were in good shape. She'd even spent a solid day chopping wood just in case they might need to start a fire.

"Good thing I did," Tai said, glaring up at the sky that was stubbornly grey.

Every so often the clouds shifted just enough that she'd get a glimpse of brightness where the sun was hidden but then the clouds huddled together, blocking the sun again. Made the forest seem like something from a fairy tail, all dark and gloomy and wet. Even the wonderful crisp scent of the cedars looming over the island didn't help. Cedar and ferns and moss-covered rocks didn't appeal when they were covered with rain drops and the wind cut right through you.

Tai bounced again.

Water soaked her shoes again.

Chibuike better have brought booze. Normally, Tai would have forbidden it, knowing that Chibuike would sneak it in anyway, but celebrating Tai's inheritance, Chibuike's new job, Abia's new commission and Xinyi's new lover Shani made a nice night of drinking and telling stories inevitable. Necessary even.

And with this stupid weather the booze would be even more welcome. Tai would just have to make sure that no one went out on the dock after dark. Too much risk of drowning and even a dip in the Sound could kill you if you didn't get warmed back up again.

"Speaking of which," Tai said as she peered around the end of the island towards the mainland, "where are they?"

Her fingers and toes really did feel like ice.

She stopped bouncing, which of course made the splashing over her poor cold feet stop just as Mother would have said if she'd still been alive to watch Tai freezing on the dock. And listened hard. Water splashing, waves a bit higher than she'd wanted for her friends' arrival. An eagle calling in the distance. The obnoxious honking rasp of a deer over on the next island over, the one that was a nature preserve with too many deer for its size but don't say that to the people back on the mainland. Hunting deer and eating them was evil.

Tai rolled her eyes. As if letting the deer starve to death was better.

Then she gasped and bounced again because there, finally, was the sound she'd been waiting for. The big boat, the one with the heavy engine that could push it through the worst chop on the Sound, was nearing the tip of the island. Give it three more minutes, max, and they'd round the point and enter Twilight Bay.

It only took two minutes for the big boat, lavender hull almost grey in this dismal light, to sail majestically around the point. Tai cheered and started waving, getting only one wave back and that from Chibuike. The others were all hunkered down, probably wrapped up in the old wool Army blankets Mother had insisted on for trips out to the island.

A good idea, if smelly. The wool did keep you warm, even when wet.

Tai's feet were wet right up to her calves by the time Chibuike and she got the big boat tied up to the dock. The others, Abia in particular, were so hunkered down under the blankets that Tai was glad that she'd heated up the hot tub last night. They all needed to get warm. Her included.

Weird part was that there was a spare person in the boat along with the others that Tai had expected. Sure, Xinyi had said that her lover Shani had a roommate who was 'having some trouble right now and in need of a break' but Tai hadn't expected the roommate to come out to the island, too. She'd sort of assumed that the roommate would be perfectly happy to have their apartment to themselves. Privacy was a lovely, lovely thing, after all.

The roommate, whatever her name was, was even lovelier so Tai couldn't help but be glad that the plans had changed. Beautiful dark skin that was mostly hidden away under a huge grey hoodie tempted Tai to introduce herself immediately but the wary look in the roommate's eyes made that a bad idea.

So.

"Come on, get out!" Tai said, grinning at them. And then groaning when Abia pulled the Army blanket up over her head. "Abia. There's a hot tub. And hot showers. And I've got the fire started. I even started a nice stew in the crock pot."

"You promised nice weather," Abia complained. Her voice was muffled by the blanket. "This is not nice weather."

"I promised a nice week of peace and quiet, not 'nice weather'," Tai countered as Xinyi started tugging the blanket out of Abia's hands while Chibuike passed one carryon suitcase and two duffle bags to Tai. "Now come on. It's way warmer inside and my toes are wet."

That got Abia up and moving, thank goodness. Trust Abia to go all Mom on Tai at the drop of a hat.

Where Abia was short, round and busty, an exact opposite to Tia's slender, flat-chested frame, Xinyi shared her body-builder's physique with her lover Shani. Who was even taller than Xinyi at an easy six two to Xinyi's five eleven. The roommate, quiet and shy and very much not even slightly Asian in descent, climbed out of the big boat and hesitantly carried duffles after Tai.

Her eyes were huge and brown as cedar wood that'd been stained, with coppery-brown hair that poofed in tiny ringlets all around her head. Not quite an afro but close. Tai stared for a second, wondering if the freckles were sun damage or natural. Then she shrugged it off and smiled at the roommate.

"Hi," Tai said as welcomingly as she possibly could because this had to be weird as all hell, going off to an island with a bunch of women she didn't know. "I'm Tai Niven, no relation to the writer. You must be Shani's roommate. I wasn't expecting you but we'll make do. You're totally welcome. Another set of hands to carry stuff up to the cabin is absolutely lovely."

"Ah, thanks?" the roommate said, staring at Tai as if she wanted to run back to the boat and sail right back to the mainland.

"This is Lake," Xinyi said, grinning at Lake as if she'd predicted just this. "Lake Nimit. I told you it'd be fine. Tai's so-called cabin has plenty of room."

"It's a cabin!" Tai protested even though all the others except Lake rolled their eyes. "Come on, guys. It's absolutely a cabin. We've got a generator for power and gas heating, cooking, everything and it's made of logs. It's a cabin."

"It's got eight bedrooms," Xinyi said to Lake whose eyes had only gotten bigger with the teasing. "A hot tub to fit ten people easily and twenty if they're cozy. And the kitchen is the sort of thing you'd see in one of those lifestyles of the rich and shameless shows."

Tai whined and drooped dramatically, almost dropping her duffels into the moss coating the shore instead of grass, but only because she wanted to see if she could get Lake to laugh. It took a moment but as Abia and Chibuike started laughing, and Shani grinned, Lake breathed a little laugh that made Tai's heart do a flip.

And no, no questioning why that flip was so pronounced. As if Tai didn't already know. So no questions, not questions at all, not a single one, especially not if Lake was single and interested in girls.

Not when there were stairs up the shore to climb, luggage to carry and a dozen stories of the trip hear for Tai to exclaim over. Thankfully, even though the afternoon was grey and gloomy, it wasn't so dark that they couldn't see their way up the path through the cedars to the cabin.

Which, no, wasn't a mansion or something. No matter what Xinyi always said when she visited. It was big, yes, and had a lot of very small bedrooms but it wasn't that huge. Every single log had come from the island. For that matter, most of the furniture had been crafted from wood harvested on the island. From the cedar chairs out on the deck to the bedframes, tables and cabinets inside, it was all native to the island.

"This is... pretty big," Lake said once Tai let everyone inside where, thank goodness, it was much, much warmer.

"Still a cabin," Tai said, bumping shoulders with Xinyi who laughed and bumped back. "Come on. Shoes off. I've got nice fuzzy slippers for everyone. The big sheepskin boots are for you, Abia. I know you're going to claim them anyway."

Tai sat down on the floor and pulled off her shoes and socks, crowing as Abia choked at the sight of water dripping off her socks. Though, granted, her toes were pretty blue. And a little numb. Not frostbitten, no, but very, very chilled.

She listened with half an ear to the lecture Abia leveled on her as Abia bustled around, getting towels to dry Tai's feet, warm socks from Tai's bedroom and then a nice big cup of tea that Shani had somehow prepared all stealth-like while the others focused on Abia and Tai.

Nice.

Shani was going to fit right in if she was the quietly motherly type. She and Abia would team up and make Tai behave in no time. Or they'd try, anyway.

Tai made sure that the others got their picks of rooms, steering Lake away from the bedroom at the far end of the cabin from the great room. That one was always cold as ice, even in the heat of the Puget Sound's brief summer. She ended up directly opposite Tai's bedroom, in the one that was decorated all in forest green and gold accents. It had the heaviest door, made of thick planks of cedar that had been carved in native Salish patterns for bear and salmon and elk.

Xinyi pulled Shani into their room, two doors up, while Chibuike and Abia pretended to argue about who'd get to have the red and the white rooms next door to Tai and Lake's rooms respectively. But they ended up exactly as they always did with Abia in the red and Chibuike in the white. Tai shook her head, grinning at Lake who hesitated in the doorway, one hand gripping the handle so hard that her knuckles were white.

"It really is okay," Tai murmured to Lake who started as if more afraid of the gentle tone than Tai's usually loud and obnoxious voice. "I didn't expect you but you're welcome here, Lake. Seriously. You don't have to hang out with us if you don't want to. Oh, but don't go out walking on the shore at night. It's super slippery and you could die really quick in the water if you fell in. The Sound's very cold. Like instant hypothermia cold. If you see the fire's gone down, toss another log on. Other than that, relax. Enjoy yourself. You can unpack or not as you choose. Dinner should be ready in a half hour or an hour. I hope you like it here."

Tai's cheeks were red by the time she managed to stop talking. Darn it all. Lake stared at her, mouth open for a long while. Then she nodded, smiled for a millisecond, and then disappeared into her room.

Tai sighed.

Just like her to be instantly smitten by someone who either wasn't interested in girls or who was so shy that Tai's personality alone would scare them away.

Oh well.

At least the others were here and they had a good long week to relax and enjoy themselves. Even if nothing happened with Lake, it should be awesome.

Though Tai couldn't help but hope, as she headed into the kitchen to start making biscuits to go with the stew, that something would come of her new little crush. Lake was lovely and Tai had been along long enough.

2. MOSSY PATH

*L*ake licked her fingers. Cheesy poof crumbs. Best thing ever. Maybe.

She didn't look into the bag lying listless and deflated by her side. The porch was cold, damp, quieter than anything Lake had ever experienced. Just blowing wind, waves off on the shores of the islands, and the sounds of birds in the trees. Not one motor anywhere. If anyone asked, she was going to blame the quiet on eating so many cheesy poofs.

First time she'd ever eaten a whole bag by herself in one sitting. She kinda felt queasy. Well, maybe more than kinda. Between the huge bowl of stew last night, with really amazing homemade bread, breakfast this morning with eggs, bacon, more amazing bread topped with six different sorts of jam, and then an enormous sandwich at lunch packed with meat and veggies, Lake had been pretty full even before she sat down with the bag of cheesy poofs.

More food than she generally ate in a week, all spread out in front of her. None of the others seemed to notice that Lake ate and ate and ate. Tai had. But she hadn't frowned or made any comments about Lake's weight or even pulled the food away.

She'd pushed it at Lake and then made more like that was a totally normal thing for someone to do for an utter stranger who'd shown up without notice to your house.

Lake's cheesy dust coated fingers shook as a chill bounced up her back, shuddering her teeth and spine.

Apparently, Shani had been right. Lake was allowed. Welcome, even. It seemed like a joke where the punchline had yet to hit. People like this didn't welcome Lake. They didn't treat her like a friend or smile when she showed up or, especially, go red and flustered and adorable when Lake looked at them.

Gramma would have said that that was because Lake always put her nose where it didn't belong. And that she was taking things that weren't hers by just being here. Of course, Gramma would have made sure that Lake didn't eat half what she had so far. There was no point to even thinking about what she'd have said or done to Lake for eating an entire bag of cheesy poofs all by herself even if Lake had spent her own money on them.

Lake bit her lip as Gramma's eternal scolding echoed in her head. Even here, a continent away, Lake couldn't get away from Gramma. Nothing was going to change. She already knew that. No matter what Lake tried, she never succeeded at anything. Every time she made an effort she ended up embarrassing herself and skulking back home to Gramma who scowled and huffed and sent her back to her room at the rear of the house with a few well-chosen words about what a waste of breath Lake was.

"Hey, there you are," Tai said, loud and bright as the brassy-loud black and white birds Shani had said were called jays. "Wondered where you went. Oh. You didn't. You ate the whole bag?"

Lake started to apologize automatically but had a delighted grin, the dopey sort that made Tai's eyes squinch up and her molars show as she bounced on her toes. Every bounce made her beaten-up track shoes squish a little as if she already had wet feet. Or was that still?

"Um. Yeah?" Lake said.

"Way to go!" Tai exclaimed. "Man, I never can resist those things. Best damn junk food in the world. Abia's making dinner so she shooed me out. And, of course, Xinyi and Shani are off in their bedroom making out. You wanna go for a walk? After a full bag like that you're going to want to walk some of it off. Otherwise Abia will make sad faces at you and do that wrist against the forehead thing like you're getting sick."

"How do you people eat so much?" Lake asked as she stood, empty bag in one hand and heart in her throat. "Seriously, I don't get it."

"Eh, food eaten on vacation has no calories," Tai said as if it was law of nature. "We all agreed early on that we're going to enjoy ourselves and good food is part of that. So no calories or diets while we're here."

She snagged the bag and calmly tossed it into a garbage bin that Lake hadn't even noticed was there. It was tucked away into a cedar planter looking thing so it was really well camouflaged. Then she bounced down the stairs, swinging her arms and smiling at the world as if it was the most beautiful thing she'd ever seen. Except that she turned and stared up at Lake as if Lake was even more beautiful.

"We've got some great walking trails on the island," Tai said. "We'll probably all go walking tomorrow. Unless it pours. Which it might. There's no TV or internet or anything out here but Abia had the radio on earlier and they said today's going to be misty in the evening but tomorrow will be really glorious. Except for a chance of rain in the afternoon. Which sucks. I wanted to go out fishing sometime this week and it's not looking like that's going to happen. You haven't eaten until you've had fresh-caught salmon straight from the Sound. So rich and just the best."

She caught Lake's hand once Lake carefully went down the slippery stairs and then they were off. Tai kept up a steady stream of chatter about the island, which had been in her mother's family for two generations, then her mother, who'd been dead for two years but who was apparently not all that missed by anyone, and the slugs.

Which.

Really?

Slugs?

"There we go!" Tai exclaimed as they emerged out onto the shore where the ridiculously lavender boat was tied up. "See? I told you the slugs could get to six inches long."

Tai pointed down towards her feet and then burst out laughing as Lake screamed and scrambled backwards away from the monster slug. Golden-green and easily as long as Lake's hand, the thing slowly slithered its way across the end of the dock, leaving behind a shimmering trail of slime.

"Oh. My. God!" Lake gasped. Her stomach tried to rebel but a hand over her mouth stopped that. For the moment.

"They're harmless," Tai said, grinning at her. "Lots of them, of course, especially at this time of the summer. A few weeks earlier and they'd have been tiny. In another couple of weeks, they'll all be gone. Don't worry about it. Worst that'll happen is that you'll step on one and slip."

"Oh gross," Lake whined. She shuddered and thought about running straight back to the cabin but there were mossy trails and dangling ferns and so many trees that those horrible slugs could be hiding behind. "That's nasty!"

"You are so not from the Puget Sound," Tai said and then burst into belly laughter that echoed over the water.

Her laughter was as bright and open as she was. There didn't seem to be a single thing that Tai hid from the world. She was as open as the water behind her, as clear as glass. Lake stared, heart beating faster from want instead of disgust at the slug.

She'd never met anyone as open as Tai was.

Or as beautiful. Slender, athletic, graceful despite her endless movement or perhaps because of it, Tai looked like a wood nymph made flesh. Except, you know, most wood nymphs probably didn't have an undercut that was dyed purple on the left side of their heads. Or battered shoes that looked like the tops were about to separate from the bottoms. Or a red and black flannel shirt that had obviously been worn so many times that it was as soft as butter in August.

Man, Lake was so crushing.

Not good.

"How about I go first and warn you of any slugs we encounter?" Tai offered once she stopped laughing with a delighted wheeze and a sunshine-bright grin up at Lake.

"Um. Deal, I think," Lake said. She cautiously slid down the mossy slope to Tai's side. "Is there anything else I should worry about on this adventure?"

"Just spiders," Tai said. Far more seriously. "We do get brown recuses up here so be very careful if you see any big spider webs. I'll be looking, of course, but I could miss them. Brown recluse bites are nothing to mess with. They can do some serious damage."

She headed left, south, away from the dock and the monster slug. Lake was more than happy to follow Tai. The trail was super slick at first, moss covered stones as round as goose eggs making every step a challenge. Tai thrust her arms out and kept on chattering as she walked like she was on a balance beam.

Lake went more slowly, more cautiously, but pretty quickly they were heading up away from the shore and onto a proper gravel-covered trail that led around the perimeter of the island. Which. Wow. Seriously a gorgeous view. The waves were slate-blue topped with whipped cream peaks. No other islands were too close on this side. The water stretched south and east and west to the mainland. Or was that an island off to the south? West had to be an island, right?

"It's beautiful, isn't it?" Tai murmured and then snickered at Lake's start of surprise. "You stopped. So I came back. I always loved this view. I used to come out here and stare every day when I was little. No diving, though. The water's not deep enough for it here. There's a great diving spot up ahead. Not that I'd recommend it today. Too cold. But maybe we'll get lucky and there'll be a super-warm day and we can all go swimming later in the week."

"I um," Lake hesitated and then spit it out in a rush because Tai stared at her wide-eyed and eager, "didn't bring a swimsuit."

Tai stared, blinked several times, and then hooted a laugh. She clapped her hands and pranced, giggling as Lake's cheeks went red. Then redder. And then so red that she felt hot from the top of her head right down to her toes.

"No way."

"Hee!"

"You swim naked?" Lake asked. Screeched, really, and man, Gramma would have smacked her for that tone of voice. "No way!"

"Your face!" Tai said, cackling. She wiped some tears away and grinned. "We sure do. Well, topless, mostly. I mean, Abia always wears a swim top. With her breasts she kind of needs to. But I always wear board shorts to swim in and nothing else on the island. I mean, with my chest what else do I need?"

She looked down at her chest, rueful smile in place that looked way too familiar to Lake. How many times had she seen that look in the mirror, especially after Gramma said something mean? A million times, easy.

"I um." Lake patted Tai's shoulder awkward as could be. "I think you look good. Fine. I mean, they're good. I'm stopping now."

Tai beamed and laughed some more as she blushed and then grabbed Lake's hand so that they could continue walking along the trail. Her fingers were like ice but confident ice. No wonder Abia fussed over Tai getting cold. The woman turned into an ice cube at the drop of a hat.

"Thank you," Tai said, skipping for a few steps. "I act all brave about going topless but then I chicken out half of the time. So if you want to wear a shirt or something, you go right ahead and do it. I mean, if we get to swim. Who knows? It might start raining and keep on raining the rest of the week."

"And... what do we do then?" Lake asked because she definitely didn't have enough books to read for a week long stay in the mansion-sized cabin.

Tai's grin took on a decidedly predatory cast as her fingers tightened around Lake's hand. "How do you feel about Uno?"

Lake stared at Tai for a long, long moment, ignoring the heavy lace-like drapes of cedar branches around them, ignoring the glimpse ahead of an isolated looking cover that must be Tai's swimming cove. She even ignored the water that dripped down her neck from a branch overhead.

"Do you want to get us all killed?" Lake hissed. "Uno? For days? That's insane! We'll all end up dead or enemies for life when the first draw four comes out!"

It was mostly a joke. Well, partly. Uno games back home were cutthroat things that had started more than a couple outright feuds in the family. Tai bellowed a laugh as she grinned and nodded enthusiastically.

"Finally!" Tai shouted at the cedar branches dripping down on them. "Someone who takes Uno seriously enough!"

Lake laughed because what else could you do? Beautiful, rich, endlessly enthusiastic and cutthroat at Uno? She'd finally met her dream girl.

Not that it was going to work out but hey. At least she could pretend for a week that it might. As Tai laughed and laughed and then pulled her onwards down the trail, Lake decided that she'd ignore the past, Gramma's pronouncements, and just enjoy herself this week.

As much as possible when it was doomed to fail the moment they left the island.

The Shores of Twilight Bay is now available at all major retailers in ebook and TPB format.

OTHER BOOKS BY MEYARI MCFARLAND:

Day Hunt on the Final Oblivion

Day of Joy

Immortal Sky

A New Path

Following the Trail

Crafting Home

Finding a Way

Go Between

Like Arrows of Fate

Out of Disaster

The Shores of Twilight Bay

Coming Together

Following the Beacon

The Solace of Her Clan

You can find these and many other books at www.MDR-Publishing.com. We are a small independent publisher focusing on LGBT content. Please sign up for our mailing list to get regular updates on the latest preorders and new releases and a free ebook!

AFTERWORD

I grew up in a canoe family. My parents would take my little brother and I out canoeing as often as they could all summer long. I learned to paddle and steer along with learning to swim, even though the Montana lakes of my childhood were snow-fed and frigid as only just-melted snow could be.

Once I finished college, I moved to the Puget Sound, which is full of gorgeous little islands and beautiful fern-draped hiking trails. Stories like this one grew in equal parts out of those childhood canoe trips and the hiking I've done as an adult.

It's always nice to get out and experience the rain and wind and weather, even when it's freezing. It's even better when you have someone you love by your side.

If you want more stories like this, please go sign up for my newsletter on www.MDR-Publishing.com or my Patreon. You'll get updates on whatever I've got coming up, special deals and you can get a free ebook or collection of my short stories.

Thank you for reading!

Meyari McFarland
   January, 2024
   www.MDR-Publishing.com

AUTHOR BIO

Meyari McFarland has been telling stories since she was a small child. Her stories range from SF and Fantasy adventures to Romances but they always feature strong characters who do what they think is right no matter what gets in their way.

Her series range from Space Opera Romance in the Drath series to Epic Fantasy in the Mages of Tindiere world. Other series include Matriarchies of Muirin, the Clockwork Rift Steampunk mysteries, and the Tales of Unification urban fantasy stories, plus many more.

You can find all of her work on MDR Publishing's website.

MORE FROM MEYARI MCFARLAND

Website:
www.MDR-Publishing.com

SOCIAL MEDIA:

Patreon - https://www.patreon.com/meyarimcfarland
Mastodon – https://wandering.shop/@MeyariMcFarland
Pillowfort - https://www.pillowfort.social/Meyari
Facebook - https://www.facebook.com/meyari.mcfarland.5
Pinterest - https://www.pinterest.com/meyarim/

If you enjoyed this story, please leave a comment on your favorite site. Also, please sign up for the newsletter so that you can hear about the latest preorders and new releases.

www.ingramcontent.com/pod-product-compliance
Lightning Source LLC
LaVergne TN
LVHW042004060526
838200LV00041B/1872